The Sourdough Man

An Alaska Folktale

Chérie B. Stihler

PAWS IV *published by* SASQUATCH BOOKS

Illustrations by Barbara Lavallee

Out on the tundra sat an old sod house.
"Qujhaaq please go catch some fish for our dinner," said Grandmother
one morning, "And I will make some bread."

Grandmother rolled the sourdough onto the table. "I will make this a sweet treat for
Qujhaaq," said Grandmother. First she added bearberries to the dough, then pulled and
squished the dough into the shape of a little man. Grandmother added two blueberries
for eyes and poked in dried cranberries for a mouth. She squeezed a few cloudberries
for a little atikluq for a body and a tiny pair of mukluks for his feet. Grandmother
brushed the Sourdough Man with butter and sprinkled sugar and cinnamon all over.

As a final touch she gave his cheeks a little pinch to make a cheery smile.

At last the Sourdough Man was ready to bake.

Wonderful smells from the oven told her that the Sourdough Man was done.

Grandmother pulled the sweet bread from the oven and set it on the table to cool.

But as she turned to pour water into the teapot, the Sourdough Man jumped off the table.

"Run as fast as the river—
Run as fast as you can,
But you won't catch me;
I'm the Sourdough Man!"

He shouted and hurried toward the door.

Grandmother ran out the door after him. She ran along the tool shed, through the vegetable garden, and past the dog yard, but she soon grew tired and had to rest.
"Oh, go on then," yelled Grandmother. "I will catch up as soon as I catch my breath."

The Sourdough Man only laughed.
He ran out onto the tundra just as fast as his little mukluks could carry him

The tundra sang with the hum of mosquitoes. Rolling waves of wind washed over the grasses.
Lupines, bluebells, and forget-me-nots sprinkled the hills with millions of spots of color.
Fresh lichens gathered around rocks.
Animals hurried to eat what they could during this season of plenty.

Musk Ox looked like a giant dandelion ready to blow away.
The wind fluffed his shaggy coat as he grazed among the tussocks.
Musk Ox looked up from his munching as a small thing drew near.

"Run as fast as the river—run as fast as you can,
 But you won't catch me; I'm the Sourdough Man!
 I ran away from Grandmother, and I can run away from you."

Musk Ox paused between mouthfuls of crunchy cotton grass and sniffed.

"You don't look like the things that I usually eat,
but that good berry smell means a sweet, tasty treat."

The Sourdough Man had already run off. Musk Ox chased after him.

Not far down the valley, the Sourdough Man ran alongside Lemming as she scurried through a patch of tundra roses. Her cheeks were stuffed with seeds.

"Run as fast as the river—run as fast as you can,
But you won't catch me; I'm the Sourdough Man!
I ran away from Grandmother.
I ran away from Musk Ox, and I can run away from you."

Lemming was too polite to answer with her mouth full. She started toward her den, but the sweet smell of the Sourdough Man's cloudberry atikluq changed her mind. She too joined the chase.

The Sourdough Man laughed and ran just as fast as his little mukluks could carry him.

He came upon Raven and Ptarmigan fighting over the last of the summer raspberries.

The Sourdough Man sang out as he passed:

"Run as fast as the river—run as fast as you can,
 But you won't catch me; I'm the Sourdough Man!
 I ran away from Grandmother.
 I ran away from Musk Ox.
 I ran away from Lemming, and I can run away from you."

"He looks tastier than your old raspberries," said Raven.

"No, you take the berries," insisted Ptarmigan.
"You don't look like the things that we usually eat,
but that good berry smell means a sweet, tasty treat."

Their raspberries lay forgotten as Raven and Ptarmigan followed the Sourdough Man too.

Arctic Hare rested in a blueberry bog.
She jumped as the Sourdough Man raced by.

"Run as fast as the river—run as fast as you can,
But you won't catch me; I'm the Sourdough Man!
I ran away from Grandmother.
I ran away from Musk Ox.
I ran away from Lemming.
I ran away from Raven and Ptarmigan, and I can run away from you."

"You are not as juicy as these willow leaves," twitched Hare.
"You don't look like the things that I usually eat,
but that good berry smell means a sweet, tasty treat."

The Sourdough Man had run off just as fast as his little
mukluks could carry him, so Hare joined the chase.

Soon the Sourdough Man came upon Caribou.

"Run as fast as the river—run as fast as you can,
  But you won't catch me; I'm the Sourdough Man!
  I ran away from Grandmother.
  I ran away from Musk Ox.
  I ran away from Lemming.
  I ran away from Raven and Ptarmigan.
  I ran away from Hare, and I can run away from you."

"Go away," grumbled Caribou. "These lichens are my favorite."
Then he lifted his head and sniffed.
"You don't look like the things that I usually eat,
but that good berry smell means a sweet, tasty treat."

The Sourdough Man had already run away again, so Caribou took off after him.

At the top of a nearby hill, Marmot enjoyed a picnic.

The Sourdough Man ran near and shouted:

"Run as fast as the river—run as fast as you can,
But you won't catch me; I'm the Sourdough Man!
I ran away from Grandmother.
I ran away from Musk Ox.
I ran away from Lemming.
I ran away from Raven and Ptarmigan.
I ran away from Hare.
I ran away from Caribou, and I can run away from you."

"I have a feast of sorrel leaves and bunchberries," snapped Marmot.
"Wait, what's that yummy smell? Cranberries?" she asked.
"Mmmm . . . you don't look like the things that I usually eat,
but that good berry smell means a sweet, tasty treat."

However, the Sourdough Man had already run off just as fast as his little mukluks
could carry him. Marmot left her picnic and ran after him.

The ground darkened as Golden Eagle swooped and swirled overhead.

The animals scattered, but the Sourdough Man only scoffed.

"Run as fast as the river—run as fast as you can,
But you won't catch me; I'm the Sourdough Man!
I ran away from Grandmother.
I ran away from Musk Ox.
I ran away from Lemming.
I ran away from Raven and Ptarmigan.
I ran away from Hare.
I ran away from Caribou.
I ran away from Marmot, and I can run away from you."

"You are barely enough of a morsel to tempt me," sneered Golden Eagle from high above.

The Sourdough Man only laughed and ran off again.

Golden Eagle circled lower this time and joined the chase.

Arctic Fox's ears wiggled as Eagle's words drifted over the hill.
He raised his nose to check the breeze, then trotted over to the cool shade
near the river and waited for that good berry smell to arrive.

The Sourdough Man soon appeared, but stopped at the river's edge.

He looked back at the animals coming down the hill. Then he looked at Fox.

"Run as fast as the river—run as fast as you can,
  But you won't catch me; I'm the Sourdough Man!
  I ran away from Grandmother.
  I ran away from Musk Ox.
  I ran away from Lemming.
  I ran away from Raven and Ptarmigan.
  I ran away from Hare.
  I ran away from Caribou.
  I ran away from Marmot.
  I ran away from Eagle, and I can run away from you."

"You have plenty of time, my friend," crooned Arctic Fox.
"Why don't you join me for a rest? The shade is nice and cool." The Sourdough Man was tired and feeling rather warm. He sat on a rock and rested too.

"The river is very fast and deep, my friend. Why not let me take you across?" asked Fox.
The animals were close by now, so the Sourdough Man hopped onto Fox's back and they started across the river.

"The water is much deeper here," warned Fox.
"You'd better climb up higher."

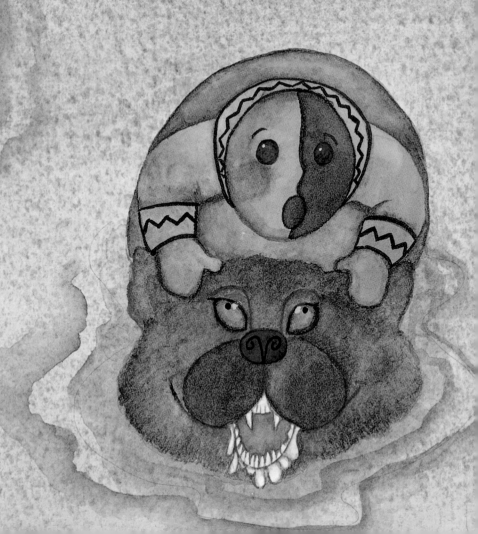

The Sourdough Man was worried about the water, so he scrambled onto Fox's head.

"Oh, look my friend. LOOK! That field of fireweed is so beautiful," said Fox.

"Where? Where? I cannot see."
The Sourdough Man leaned from side to side.

He was so excited he did not notice the many sharp teeth in Fox's mouth.

He paid no attention to the drool that dripped from Fox's jaws.

"But you must see it my friend! Crawl out on my nose for a better view," suggested Fox.

The Sourdough Man scrambled onto Fox's nose. He stood on tiptoe.

"Keep looking my friend," said Fox.

As Fox spoke his nose bounced up and down.

"Oh please, STOP my friend!
I might tumble into the river,"
squeaked the Sourdough Man.

But Fox chattered on and on.

The Sourdough Man tripped.

Then he flipped,

and slipped right into Fox's waiting mouth.

CHOMP!

Fox smiled as he chewed on his yummy treat. Refreshed from his swim, Fox trotted back to the bushes for a nap. He dreamed of his tasty snack.

Qujhaaq returned to the old sod house with fish for dinner. "Grandmother," he called, "I just saw the strangest thing. A fox paddled into the river with a loaf of bread on his nose. I ran over to get a better look, but before I could he swallowed it up."

Grandmother smiled. She pulled a fresh loaf of sourdough bread out of the oven. She was saving the story of the Sourdough Man for after dinner and was very pleased to know how the story should end.

Alaska's Sourdough Past

The history of sourdough goes back a long way—people in ancient Egypt used it more than 6,000 years ago! Sourdough was probably discovered when wild yeast drifted into some dough. The bread baked from that dough had a lighter texture and better taste. From then on, wherever people traveled, they took their sourdough along.

Westward pioneers carried the sourdough tradition throughout the United States. They called it "sponge." It traveled with the Stampeders to Alaska and into western Canadian territories during the Klondike Gold Rush.

Since sourdough starters need to be kept warm, experienced miners and other settlers frequently carried a pouch of starter either around their necks or on a belt. These starters were fiercely guarded. Long-timers in the gold camps came to be called "sourdoughs," a term that is still applied to Alaskan old-timers today.

Make Your Own Sourdough Starter

Combine 1 cup warm water (110 to 115 degrees F) with 2¼ teaspoons active dry yeast and 1½ cups flour in a 4-cup glass or plastic container. The mixture will be thick. Cover the container loosely with plastic wrap. Let it stand in a warm place (70 to 80 degrees F is perfect) for 1 to 3 days. Stir the mixture 2 or 3 times each day. Never allow any form of metal, such as a spoon or lid, to come into direct contact with the starter. Always use a plastic or wooden spoon.

Every 24 hours, throw away half of the mixture and then add ½ cup flour and ½ cup water. Within 3 or 4 days you should see lots of bubbles throughout. The mix will have a pleasant sour smell. The starter may begin to puff up, too. This is good! When your starter develops a bubbly froth, it is ready!

Keep the sourdough starter in your refrigerator with a lid covering it. Allow a little breathing space in the lid. If you're using a glass jar, ask a big person to punch a hole in the lid with a nail to allow gas to escape. After your starter has bubbled and is in the refrigerator, you only need to "feed" it once a week. To "feed" your starter, leave at least 1 cup mixture in the container, then stir in 1 cup warm water (110 to 115 degrees F) and 1½ cups flour. *Note: The amounts you take away and add to the starter are different now!* Cover loosely and let stand in a warm place for 12 hours. The starter can then be used or returned to the refrigerator.

As the starter gets older, the flavor will become tangier; baked products made with "aged" starters will have more sourdough flavor. The starter serves as the leavening, so no additional yeast is needed.

For a gluten-free Sourdough Starter, use white rice flour.

A most heartfelt **thank you** to the SCBWI Alaska Fairbanks folks who read *The Sourdough Man*
in every incarnation from muktuk to muffins . . . and still believed in it anyway. You all are the best!
And as always to Scott: "Olives!"
—*Chérie*

For Alex—my sweet, tasty treat.
—*Barbara*

Manufactured in China in January 2010 by C&C Offset Printing Co. Ltd. Shenzhen,
   Guangdong Province
Published by Sasquatch Books
Distributed by PGW/Perseus
15 14 13 12 11 10   10 9 8 7 6 5 4 3 2 1

Cover illustrations: Barbara Lavallee
Cover design: Rosebud Eustace
Interior illustrations: Barbara Lavallee
Interior design and composition: Rosebud Eustace
Editor: Michelle Roehm McCann

Library of Congress Cataloging-in-Publication Data is available.
ISBN-10: 1-57061-594-2
ISBN-13: 978-1-57061-594-8

Sasquatch Books
119 South Main Street, Suite 400
Seattle, WA 98104
(206) 467-4300
www.sasquatchbooks.com
custserv@sasquatchbooks.com